Other books by Pamela Allen

Mr Archimedes' Bath
Who Sank the Boat?
Bertie and the Bear
A Lion in the Night
Herbert and Harry
Mr McGee
Mr McGee Goes to Sea
Fancy That!
I Wish I Had a Pirate Suit
My Cat Maisie
Black Dog

HAMISH HAMILTON CHILDREN'S BOOKS
Published by the Penguin Group
27 Wrights Lane, London W8 5TZ, England
Penguin Books USA Inc, 375 Hudson Street, New York, New York 10014, U.S.A.
Penguin Books Australia Ltd, Ringwood, Victoria, Australia
Penguin Books Canada Ltd, 10 Alcorn Avenue, Toronto, Ontario, Canada M4V 3B2
Penguin Books (NZ) Ltd, 182–190 Wairau Road, Auckland 10, New Zealand

Penguin Books Ltd, Registered Offices: Harmondsworth, Middlesex, England

First Published in Great Britain 1993 by Hamish Hamilton Ltd
First Published in Australia 1992 by Viking Australia

Text and illustrations copyright © 1992 by Pamela Allen

1 3 5 7 9 10 8 6 4 2

The moral right of the author has been asserted

British Library Cataloguing in Publication Data
CIP data for this book is available from the British Library

ISBN 0-241-13306.8

Designed by Deborah Brash/Brash Design Pty Ltd, Sydney
Typeset in Palatino by Post Typesetters, Brisbane
Made and printed in Hong Kong through Bookbuilders Limited

BELINDA

BELINDA

Pamela Allen

HAMISH HAMILTON • LONDON

Bessie and Old Tom live in the country.

Early every morning Old Tom works
in his garden.
There is always plenty to do.
He grows cucumbers and carrots.
He grows pumpkins and parsley.
He grows beetroot and beans,
and lots of other vegetables.

Early every morning Bessie milks
Belinda the cow.
There is always plenty of milk.
She gives some to the dog.
She gives some to the cat.
She puts some aside for Old Tom
and herself.

With the cream she makes
the butter for their bread,
and the skimmed milk
she gives to the pig.

ONE DAY Bessie packed her bag,
put on her hat and coat
and went to stay with her daughter
who lived in the city.
She left Old Tom to milk Belinda the cow,
make the butter, and feed the dog,
the cat, and the pig.

So the next morning
Old Tom was up very VERY early.
He took the bucket and the stool
and set out to find Belinda.
Belinda was chewing in the far corner
of the paddock.
He sat on the stool and placed the bucket
carefully between his knees.
Gently he put his hand on her teat.
'There's a good girl,' he crooned.

Belinda gave one almighty kick.

Old Tom flew high in the air
and landed with a thud in the mud.

Belinda was off . . .
and Old Tom was off after her.

Around and around they went.
Mooing and trotting, mooing and trotting,
around and around and *around* they went,
until Old Tom was quite out of breath.

What *was* Old Tom to do?
There would be no milk for the dog,
no milk for the cat, no milk for the pig,
no milk for Old Tom
and no butter for his bread.

What WAS old Tom to do?

He went to the shed and
took a rope from the wall.
Then he went to his garden
and pulled up the biggest,
fattest carrot he could find.

With these he set out to catch Belinda.

'Moooooooooooooooo!' crooned Old Tom.
'There's a pretty girl. Fat carrot, fat carrot.
Come... Come to Old Tom. There's a good girl.'

'Moooooooooooooooo!' answered Belinda as she cautiously, carefully inched towards the carrot.

'MoooooOOOOOOOoooo!' bellowed Belinda
as she snatched the carrot from
Old Tom's outstretched hand.

'OooooooOOOOOOOOOooo!' cried old Tom
as he landed with a thud in the mud.

Belinda took off . . .
and Old Tom took off after her.
Around and around they went.
Mooing and trotting, mooing and trotting,
around and around and *around* they went,
until Old Tom was quite out of breath.

Now what was Old Tom to do?

If he couldn't catch Belinda,
he couldn't milk Belinda,
and if he couldn't milk Belinda
there would be no milk for the dog,
no milk for the cat, no milk for the pig,
no milk for Old Tom and no butter for his bread.

What WAS Old Tom to do?

He thought   and thought   and thought

and thought   and thought.

At last he stood up and strode into the house.

He took Bessie's pink dress from the wardrobe
and put it on.
The dress was too big.
So he took a pillow from the bed
and pulled and pushed, and stuffed and shoved,

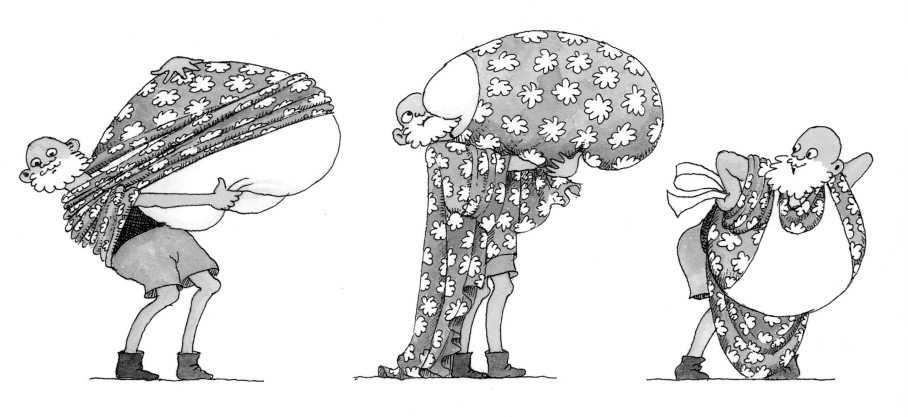

until at last the pillow was with him inside the dress.
Then he tied Bessie's apron firmly around his middle to hold everything in place.

He put on Bessie's big straw hat
and he pulled on Bessie's big rubber boots.

In this disguise he set out to milk Belinda.

Belinda was chewing in the
far corner of the paddock.
She looked up, blinked, then went on chewing.
Quietly Old Tom came closer and closer.

He sat on the stool.
He placed the bucket
carefully between his knees
Gently he put his hand on her teat.
This time Old Tom didn't say a word.

He squeezed.

A warm white spray made a ping
in the empty bucket. He tried again.

Squi..............rt, squi..............rt.
Squi..............rt, squi..............rt.
Squi..............rt, squi..............rt.

The milk crept up and up
until the bucket was full
and no more milk would come.

Now there was plenty of milk.
There was milk for the dog.
There was milk for the cat.
There was milk for Old Tom
and cream to make the butter for his bread.

There was even plenty of skimmed milk
left for the pig.

When Bessie came home she wondered how
her pink dress came to have mud on the hem.
She almost said,
'Who's been wearing my dress?'
but Old Tom had been the only one at home.

And it couldn't have been Old Tom
— could it?